Warbler

Hummingbird

Hawk

Sparrow

Chickadee

Christie Matheson

BIRD WATCH

Greenwillow Books

An Imprint of HarperCollinsPublishers

Bird Watch
Copyright © 2019 by Christie Matheson.
All rights reserved. Manufactured in China.
For information address HarperCollins Children's Books,
a division of HarperCollins Publishers, 195 Broadway, New York, NY 10007.
www.harpercollinschildrens.com

Watercolor paints and collages were used to prepare the full-color art.
The text type is 30-point Venetian 301 BT.

Library of Congress Cataloging-in-Publication Data is available.

ISBN 978-0-06-239340-1 (hardback)

First Edition
19 20 21 22 23 SCP 10 9 8 7 6 5 4 3 2 1

Greenwillow Books

For Kerri

*"Always be on the lookout
for the presence of wonder."*
—*E. B. White*

BIRDING CHECKLIST

Chickadee

Warbler

Bluebird

Dove

Sparrow

Hummingbird

Wren

Hawk

Robin

Owl

There are treasures hiding in the trees
and on the ground and in the air.

If you go outside and look carefully,
you just might find them.

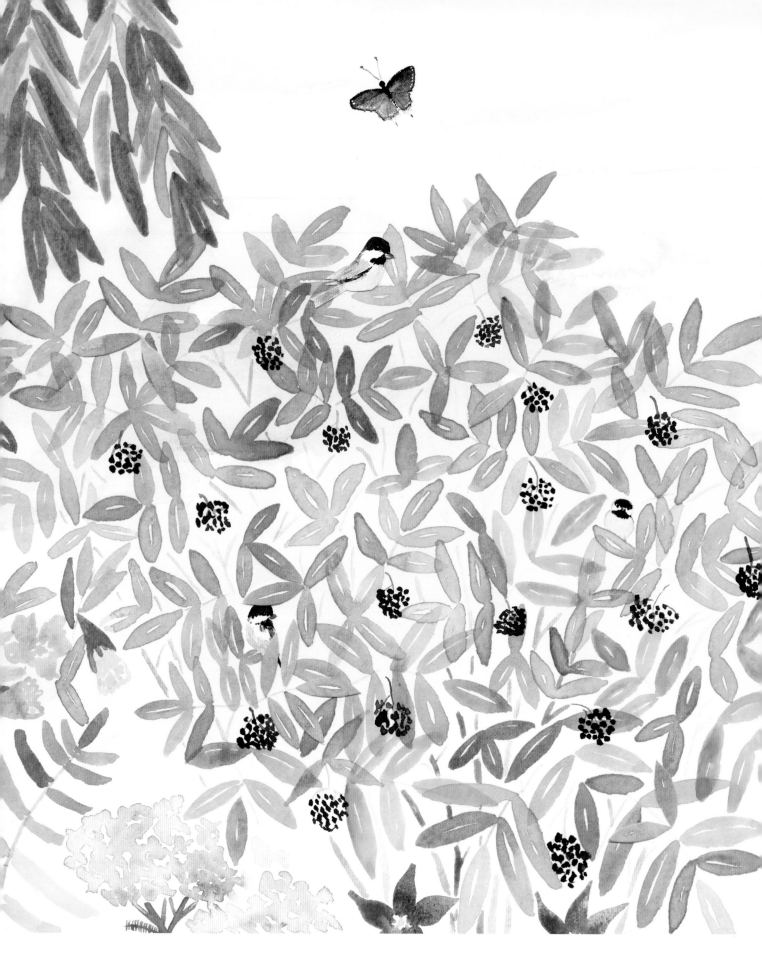

On a beautiful morning, you just might find
ten black-capped chickadees perching in the trees.

They are your first treasure!
Do you see them all?

As the chickadees fly away, you just might find nine bluebirds landing nearby.

Their feathers look mostly blue—
but some have orange feathers, too.

If you look closely, you just might find
eight sparrows hiding near the ground.

Make a wish and *whoosh!*
Blow on the dandelions.

It's a seed feast!

As a few raindrops fall,
you just might find seven wrens singing.

Try to spy their stripy tails.

While the wrens take cover,
you just might find
six robins looking for worms.

Aha!

One has a worm in her beak already.

When the blue sky returns, you just
might find five sunny yellow warblers.

Well, there's one. Could there be more?
Turn the page and you just might find . . .

another warbler!

Now there are two.
But where are the other three?

While you wait for more warblers,
you just might find a bee, a spider,

a red ladybug, a delicate dragonfly,
and a slimy banana slug.

As the slug slinks along,
you just might find four doves cooing.

Count them quietly,
so you don't scare them away.

Near the brightest flowers,
you just might find three hummingbirds hovering.

They are searching for nectar to sip.

While the hummingbirds snack,
mice scurry about. How many can you see?

Uh-oh. You just might find
two hawks eyeing those mice.

The hawks are soaring away!
Can you see the hummingbird
who zipped up to tease them?

She is tiny.
And the hawks just found
that she is very brave.

When the sky grows darker,
you just might find one more beautiful bird.

Who could it be?
Turn the page to see.

That's who!

Most of the birds are sleeping now,
though the owl may be up all night.

But if you look again in the morning,
you just might find...

the treasure you've been waiting for.

More About Birds and Birding

You can go bird-watching—which is also simply called birding—almost anywhere and anytime. Birds live in and visit lots of places outdoors: yards, parks, woods, open fields, and even busy city sidewalks. But as in this book, they are not always in plain sight.

To find birds, start by listening. Sometimes it helps to close your eyes and "look" with your ears only. If you hear any chirping or tweeting or singing, birds are probably nearby. Then watch! Be patient. A movement in a tree or on the ground or streaking through the sky could be a bird. When you spot one, look closely, and see if you can identify it.

You can attract birds by hanging a bird feeder filled with birdseed somewhere outside. When birds come to eat, you can watch them from outside or through your window.

Healthy birds are good for us and for the planet. They pollinate plants, spread seeds, and are part of the natural life cycle. They connect people to nature and are a visible and important reminder that humans are not the only creatures inhabiting the earth. Protecting bird environments means protecting the world as a whole. And people who appreciate birds are a lot more likely to help take care of the place where we all live.

Some of my favorite resources for learning about birds are the *National Geographic Kids Bird Guide of North America*, *The Young Birder's Guide to Birds of North America* from Peterson Field Guides, the Sibley Backyard Birding Flashcards, the All About Birds website from the Cornell Lab of Ornithology (www.allaboutbirds.org), and the National Audubon Society website (www.audubon.org).

There are ten different bird species in this book, all common in North America (and many can also be found around the world). Here are some interesting facts about each of them.

Chickadees: The chickadees in this book are black-capped chickadees, so named because of their cute black heads. They eat insects, seeds, and berries, and often hide seeds in trees to eat later. These smart little birds can remember thousands of hiding places.

Bluebirds: The bluebirds in this book are western bluebirds, which are similar to eastern bluebirds. Females of both types tend to be blue and gray, while males have bright blue heads and wings and rusty orange breasts. Bluebirds are very social, and when you see one it is likely to be in a flock with other bluebirds.

Sparrows: The sparrows in this book are white-crowned sparrows, which eat mainly seeds that they find near the ground, in areas with lots of low foliage (that's another word for plants). Sparrows usually migrate, which means they live in one place during the summer and move to a warmer place for the winter. When they are migrating, some white-crowned sparrows travel hundreds of miles in a single night.

Wrens: The wrens in this book are house wrens. They have that name because they often nest in cavities near people's houses, or in birdhouses. But they can be found in many places with trees and bushes. A male house wren builds several nests using twigs, and the female wren chooses the one she likes best and finishes it with soft materials, such as feathers and grass.

Robins: Robins are known for eating worms, and they do, but they also love to eat fruit. In fact, more than half their diet consists of fruit, mostly berries. But robin parents mainly feed their babies worms and insects.

Warblers: The warblers in this book are yellow warblers. Females build nests for their eggs, making a cup out of grass and bark and lining it with soft feathers, animal hair, and plant fibers. They lay one to seven eggs at a time. Yellow warbler babies are tiny, weighing about 1/20 of an ounce when they are born.

Doves: The doves in this book are mourning doves. They eat mostly seeds, which they find on or near the ground and then swallow and store in a place in their throat called a *crop*. When they have stored all the seeds they can, they go to a safe place, such as a tree branch, where they are somewhat hidden from view, to digest their meal.

Hummingbirds: The hummingbirds in this book are Anna's hummingbirds. They drink nectar from flowers, and they eat insects and tree sap. Tiny hummingbirds can beat their wings as fast as 200 times per *second*, and they weigh less than a nickel. But you might occasionally see them chasing much larger birds away—it's an instinct to protect their territory.

Hawks: The hawks in this book are red-tailed hawks, the most common species of hawk in North America. They eat small animals such as mice, voles, and squirrels. Adult red-tailed hawks don't have many predators, but sometimes smaller birds—such as hummingbirds—chase them out of an area.

Owls: The owl in this book is a great horned owl. Owls are usually nocturnal, which means they are most active at night. Great horned owls have very big eyes and good vision in the dark. Instead of moving their eyes, owls swivel their heads to look in any direction. They also have excellent hearing.

Bluebird

Dove

Wren

Owl

Robin